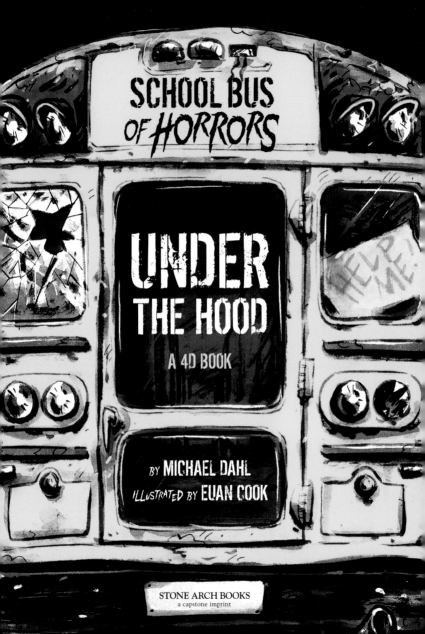

SCHOOL BUS
OF HORRORS

UNDER
THE HOOD

A 4D BOOK

BY MICHAEL DAHL

ILLUSTRATED BY EUAN COOK

HELP! ME!

STONE ARCH BOOKS
a capstone imprint

School Bus of Horrors is published by
Stone Arch Books
A Capstone Imprint
1710 Roe Crest Drive
North Mankato, Minnesota 56003
www.mycapstone.com

Cataloging-in-Publication Data is available at the Library of Congress website.
ISBN 978-1-4965-6270-8 (library binding)
ISBN 978-1-4965-6276-0 (paperback)
ISBN 978-1-4965-6282-1 (eBook PDF)

Summary: A young boy rides the bus to school. Suddenly, a monstrous creature
claws at the bus's hood! It rips apart the engine! Can the boy stop the creature before
this bus ride becomes a nightmare?

Designer: Bob Lentz
Production Specialist: Tori Abraham

Cover background by Shutterstock: schankz, Nicku

Printed in the United States of America.
PA021

Download the Capstone app!

- Ask an adult to download the Capstone 4D app.

- Scan the cover and stars inside the book for additional content.

When you scan a spread, you'll find
fun extra stuff to go with this book!
You can also find these things
on the web at www.capstone4D.com
using the password: hood.62708

TABLE OF CONTENTS

From dawn to dusk, the **SCHOOL BUS OF HORRORS** rumbles along city streets and down country roads, searching for another passenger. Yellow, black markings, dirty windows—it looks like any other.

But **BEWARE!** Step aboard this bus and experience the scariest ride of your life . . .

CHAPTER ONE
A BAD START

"This stinks!" says Aaron, standing in the rain.

He waits without an umbrella at the bus stop.

He flips up his hoodie to keep his hair dry.

A strange bus arrives at Aaron's
stop.

It is not the regular bus that takes
him to school.

When it slows, the wheels splash water up from the street.

Aaron's face gets soaked. His glasses slide off his nose.

Aaron searches for his glasses on the ground.

CRUNCH!

He steps on the frames.

They split in two.

"Could this day get any worse?"
Aaron asks himself.

CHAPTER TWO
SHADOW SHAPE

Aaron stomps onto the bus, carrying his broken glasses.

He is wet and angry.

He sits down in the front seat. It is the only empty seat left.

The door closes, the engine revs up, and then the bus heads down the street.

Aaron stuffs his broken glasses
into his bag. He can barely see
anything without them.

He stares out the wet windshield
and notices a shadow.

The shadow slinks out from under
the hood. It sits on the hood like a
big, black garbage bag.

Aaron watches as a thin shape stretches out from the lump.

It looks like an arm. A long, hairy arm!

The end of the arm is shaped like a claw.

Aaron stares.

The shadowy claw seems to be holding a hammer.

"Hey, what is that?" Aaron says.

A sign blinks on above him.

Aaron squints to read it: "DO NOT TALK TO THE DRIVER."

The bus driver sits inside a plastic safety wall.

On the wall is a small opening.

The driver's wrinkled hand pokes through the opening.

The hand points up at the sign.

Aaron keeps staring out the windshield.

"Can't you see that?" he says to the plastic wall.

The clawlike hand rises again from the shadowy lump.

Then the arm swings down hard.

BANG! The hammer strikes the hood of the bus.

CHAPTER THREE
HAMMER

Aaron screams, and the other students stare at him.

"What's your problem?" asks a girl across the aisle.

"Look on the hood!" says Aaron.

He grips a nearby pole and stands, still looking out the window.

The girl across the aisle ignores him.

Aaron pulls one half of his broken glasses from his bag.

He holds the lens up to his eye.

The shadow is clearer now.

It is a creature, with long arms and suction feet. Its fur shines in the falling rain.

BANG! BANG!

The hammer hits the hood again and again.

CHAPTER FOUR
THE MONSTER

"Can't you hear that?" shouts Aaron.

The sign lights up again: "DO NOT TALK TO THE DRIVER."

As Aaron watches, the creature tears off half of the metal hood.

The shadow shape reaches its long arms down inside the hood.

Sparks fly out from the motor.

Aaron sees the hairy claws pulling long, rubbery wires.

The bus is going to crash! thinks Aaron. *The driver has to stop!*

Aaron jumps up from his seat.

He hurls himself at the plastic wall surrounding the driver.

He shoves his arm through the opening.

Aaron grabs the steering wheel.

"Stop the bus!" he shouts.

The bus comes to a sudden stop.

Aaron stumbles down the stairs and out the exit door.

He sees figures walking on the sidewalks around him.

Many of them hold umbrellas.

"Help!" he shouts. "There's a monster on the bus!"

The figures stop and lower their umbrellas.

They are not human.

They are all hairy creatures with long arms and suction feet.

A small creature holding its mother's hand points at Aaron and screams.

"It's a monster!" the mother creature shouts.

Aaron starts to run.

The creatures chase after him, growling angrily.

As Aaron flees, his head slips out from under his hoodie.

His hair is quickly soaked. But now Aaron barely even notices.

GLOSSARY

AISLE (ILE)—the passage the runs between a row of seats

CREATURE (KREE-chur)—a living thing, human or animal

HOODIE (HUD-ee)—a jacket with a hood that covers a person's head

REVS (REVZ)—makes an engine run quickly and noisily

SUCTION (SUKT-shun)—a thin, rubbery cup that sticks to things

UMBRELLA (uhm-BREL-uh)—a folding frame with cloth stretched over it that is used to protect against rain

DISCUSS

1. Why do you believe the author titled this book *Under the Hood*?

2. At the beginning of the story, the rain bothered Aaron. At the end, he didn't even notice it. What changed?

3. In chapter one, Aaron says, "Could this day get any worse?" By the end of the story, how do you think he would answer this question? Explain.

WRITE

1. Create a new title for this book. Then write a paragraph on why you chose your new title.

2. Draw a picture of a scary monster. Then give your monster a name and write a story about it.

3. Write about the scariest bus ride you've ever experienced.

AUTHOR

MICHAEL DAHL is the author of the best-selling Library of Doom series, the Dragonblood books, and Michael Dahl's Really Scary Stories. (He wants everyone to know that last title was not his idea.) He was born a few minutes after midnight of April Fool's Day in a thunderstorm, has survived various tornados and hurricanes, as well as an attack from a rampant bunny at night ("It reared up at me!"). He currently lives in a haunted house and once saw a ghost in his high school. He will never ride on a school bus. These stories will explain why.

ILLUSTRATOR

EUAN COOK is an illustrator from London, who enjoys drawing pictures for books and watching foxes and jays out his window. He also likes walking around looking at broken brickwork, sooty statues, and the weird drainpipes and stuff you can find behind old run-down buildings.

SCHOOL BUS OF HORRORS

FRIDAY NIGHT HEADLIGHTS

DESTRUCTION ZONE

DEAD END

UNDER THE HOOD

THE SQUEALS ON THE BUS

CRUSH HOUR